"Rubinstein gathers his language ready-mades on index cards (commonplace expressions, overheard statements, sentence fragments), and then organizes them in such a way that we seem to be observing the creation of a poem from raw material. However, we are left to build our own context in which to combine these disparate elements into a meaningful whole."

Gerald Janacek, University of Kentucky

"Rubinstein's texts undermine our faith in the independence of our judgement thereby posing the difficult question of our linguistic identity. In order to speak for ourselves we must overcome 'the Other' in ourselves, but this is not at all simple. The Other has already said so much: all of our oral and written literature, all that has been accumulated over the millennia of 'speaking man' belongs to him."

Michael Epstein, Emory College

"Rubinstein juxtaposes different styles and finds them all wanting. He tries them on for size, offering numerous variants of the same thought in an attempt to establish their possibilities. He shows the relativism and the limits of any utterance, and in the pauses created by his index-card device, we become equally aware of the impossibility of expressing ourselves adequately and in full." Critic Andrei Zorin

GLAS NEW RUSSIAN WRITING
a series of contemporary Russian
writing in English translation

Volume 27

Lev Rubinstein
Лев Рубинштейн

Translated by Joanne Turnbull

Here I Am
Я здесь

Performance Poems

glas[27]

NEW RUSSIAN WRITING

The Editors of the Glas series
Natasha Perova & Arch Tait & Joanne Turnbull

Designed by Andrei Bondarenko
Typeset by Tatiana Shaposhnikova

For ordering information go to:

www.russianpress.com/glas

www.russianwriting.com

ISBN 5-7172-0058-7

Contents

Introduction

Legend has it that a lack of typing paper led to the invention of Lev Rubinstein's unique poetic and performance style. Index cards, on the other hand, abounded in the Moscow public library where he worked for some twenty years when the Soviet Union still existed. Rubinstein typed out separate lines or verses on these cards and organized them in long boxes, sometimes inserting blank cards to indicate meaningful pauses. "What is the purpose of this 'card system' for me?" says Rubinstein. "Primarily it is a material metaphor for my understanding of the text as an object, as a three-dimensional unit, and of reading as a movement into the depths, a sequential removal and overcoming of layers, a metaphor for my understanding of reading as a labor, as spectacle, and a game."

Born in 1947, Rubinstein studied language and literature at Moscow University. He first made a name for himself in the '70s as a central figure in the Moscow conceptualist movement. Needless to say, his unorthodox poems were not printed in the official literary journals of the time, but circulated instead in *samizdat*, in little cardboard boxes or ring-bound. At the same time, Rubinstein began performing his poetry in private settings for audiences of one to a dozen people. Not until the early '90s did his poems begin appearing in Russia's "thick journals". The acclaim was instant. But the standardized format meant sacrificing Rubinstein's preferred form of presentation: text fragments — a line of verse, a theoretical remark, a bit of descriptive prose, snippets of phone conversation, a stage direction, an expletive — on separate index cards.

Art directors experimented with boxes on a page, or even actual cardboard boxes filled with cards. But most chose instead to use numbers to indicate the original 3×5 cards. Meanwhile Rubinstein's performances became more frequent and the venues public with audiences into the hundreds. A short, wiry man with a scraggly gray beard and a perpetually hoarse voice, Rubinstein has an unassuming manner that at first, deceptively, suggests a lack of confidence and even a lack of familiarity with the cards he is holding uncertainly in his hands. One often gets the feeling that he is about to shuffle them — a trick that never fails to enlist his listeners as willing co-authors. Rubinstein's talent for engaging both new and long familiar audiences has caused his popularity to endure and grow through the last decade, despite the upheaval in post-Soviet tastes and cultural priorities.

Rubinstein catalogues remarkable speech fragments, disjointed bits of various discourses and staggeringly bad "traditional" rhymed poetry. These found objects he presents as poems which the reader or listener feels he must have heard somewhere hundreds of times before without noticing. "Each card is a universal unit of rhythm equal to any vocal gesture. A pack of cards is a non-book, an object of verbal culture existing outside the Gutenbergian realm."

Rubinstein's fragments invariably elicit a series of associations in any reader or listener, even one who fails to catch the various allusions. As a result, these brief texts have a modern universality that cannot be lost even in translation. Critic Ekaterina Degot likens Rubinstein's work to computer hypertexts where each message conceals a larger context and where one is necessarily forced to choose some of the many possible connections over others. She describes his poetics as that of "fatally missed opportunities". This quality has prompted other critics to compare Rubinstein's work to Chekhov's.

"The artistic system which I profess," Rubinstein explains, "deals not so much with language as with consciousness. Or rather with the complex interrelationships between individual artistic consciousness and mass cultural consciousness. In conceptualist art, the center of gravity tends to be somewhere between the author, the text and the reader: the text is as important as, but no more dominant than, the other two participants in this creative act." That makes Rubinstein's work an ongoing interactive process in which this book — the first such collection in English translation — represents the next logical step.

The editors

introduction

POETRY LIBRARY

lev rubinstein

A Catalogue of
Каталог
Comical Novelties
комедийных новшеств

lev rubinstein

[1]   You could always do something;

[2]   You could try to establish a conceptual
      unity and spend almost all your time
      on it;

[3]   You could look for connections between
      cause and effect and forget about
      everything else;

[4]   You could act as intermediary between
      the one who's leading and the one
      who's being led and not know which
      result should be considered positive;

[5]   You could classify possibilities
      according to their degree of comicality;

[6]   You could classify passions according
      to the dimensions of their consequences;

[7]   You could classify pronouncements
      according to their contextual
      significance;

[8]   You could classify people's actions
      according to their contextual
      justification;

[9]   You could classify conditions according
      to the degree of their nebulousness;

●❶❸

[10]   You could classify events according
       to foreordination;

[11]   You could classify situations according
       to the degree of their hopelessness;

[12]   You could classify doubts according
       to the degree of their irresolvable-
       ness;

[13]   You could dispel any life's doubts if
       you could only find powerful, cycle-
       generating factor — but that's just
       the problem;

lev rubinstein

[14]   You could also do something else
       without going into too much detail
       about it;

[15]   You could begin with anything at all
       in the confidence that any beginning
       is bound to be promising;

[16]   You could absolutize a momentary
       weakness by catapulting it into the
       role of a constructive principle;

[17]   You could take any feeling — apprehen-
       sion, for instance — to cosmic
       extremes;

[18]   You could enjoy all accidentally
       granted rights without openly
       declaring them;

[19]   You could teach a lesson in great
       patience and do it in such a way that
       no one even felt it;

[20] You could sponge on the border between self-mystification and self-exposure and stop to think for a minute before the bounds of decency;

[21] You could stop before the bounds of decency to consider the so-called consequences;

[22] You could stop before the need to choose or you could cross the threshold of imaginary need;

●①⑦

[23]   You could get ahead of events, but
        you could never foresee them;

[24]   You could think of everything down to
        the last detail, but you could also
        not do that;

[25]   You could wander in the wilds of
        sensory experience, following only
        false signs and ideas;

[26]   You could wander in a conceptual forest
        without giving any thought at all to
        the real purpose of your journey;

[27]   You could begin to see clearly the
       mainsprings of various phenomena and
       not tell anyone;

[28]   You could preach what you didn't
       practice, and vice versa, without any
       risk of exposure;

[29]   You could just as well take one for
       the other and take delight in your
       discovery without any risk of falling
       into error;

[30] You could just as well replace one with the other without any risk of falling into ethical heresies;

[31] You could very well feed on the energy of a secret longing;

[32] You could not look anywhere, but see everything;

[33] You could see everything, but not understand anything;

[34] You could see everything and understand everything;

[35] You could not notice anything at all; or you could, on the contrary, notice everything; or you could only notice what seems most important;

[36] You could see yourself from the outside in a dream and in such an unsavory role that you woke up out of embarrassment and shame — but that's a private matter;

[37] You could, when you saw yourself from the outside, be horrified, or you could be glad;

[38]   You could avoid people, their eyes,
        their conversations and so on, but
        wouldn't it be better to meet fate
        halfway;

[39]   You could construct mythological
        situations almost without thinking;

[40]   You could find yourself in a more
        than ambiguous situation;

[41]   You could find yourself around the
        corner and drop by for a cup of tea
        and a chat;

[42] You could talk about anything at all for as long as you liked, showing interest only in the actual texture of the speech;

[43] You could perfectly well pass the time without any risk of boring each other, but you need to know how;

[44] You could try to scare each other with all sorts of sinister allusions and achieve only the opposite;

[45] You could scrutinize each other to the point that it might turn into a fairly absorbing sort of game;

[46] You could talk about the same thing for hours, without feeling surfeited, but it would be hard;

[47] You could talk about nothing at all for hours and then say goodbye as if nothing had happened;

[48] You could stop the conversation you started once and for all and then see what came of it;

[49] You could assume that certain questions will always remain open;

[50] You could complicate everything just as you could simplify everything to such a degree that there wasn't anything left to talk about;

[51] You could so mystify your listener that the very possibility of demystification became frankly unrealistic;

[52]   You could become so tired of each
        other that new and mysterious
        incentives to communicate appeared;

[53]   You could easily get by without helping
        each other directly: silent agreement
        would be enough;

[54]   You could with endless pleasure listen
        in on other people's conversations,
        rejoicing in your success as if it
        were a personal achievement;

lev rubinstein

[55] You could resort to various contrivances so that your joy might truly know no bounds;

[56] You could get together to discuss the situation;

[57] You could get together to decide which is greater:
    — the need for a breakthrough to a new metaphysical reality or the pathological fear of making a false move;
    — a speculative understanding of the way out of the automated sphere or an emotional attachment to it;

    — a clear sense of freedom of choice or the urge to recognize the will of the usurper;
    — the voice of longed-for calm or something else;
    — and so on;

●27

[58]   You could talk about the danger of
       multifariousness when passed off as
       multiflorousness;

[59]   You could compare notes forever, but
       that wouldn't necessarily prove
       anything;

[60]   You could talk in earnest only about
       the idea of productiveness, but who
       knows what that really means;

[61] You could discuss all this with no more and no less seriousness than the subject deserves;

[62] You could suddenly imagine that a final solution had been found, but that's just what you need to watch out for;

[63] You could suddenly cast your eye on one of the countless manifestations of reality and then designate this a randomly chosen object;

[64]   You could suddenly announce for all
        the world to hear what you couldn't
        bring yourself to say even in
        confidence;

[65]   You could feel suddenly ashamed of
        what you'd said and try to make up
        for it with what you said next;

[66]   You could, without fanfare or false
        modesty, suddenly announce your own
        insolvency but that would be, in the
        first place, almost impossible and,
        in the second, absolutely uncalled-
        for;

[67] You could express your last wish, in essence, but in such a strange manner that the same thing crossed everyone's mind;

[68] You could, by just throwing someone's name out, suddenly make everyone look at each other;

[69] You could suddenly touch someone and win them over with some perfectly trivial observation;

[70]   You could talk all sorts of nonsense
        and not worry about the impression it
        made;

[71]   You could go on and on straying from
        the subject and coming back to it,
        but without stooping to any sort of
        generalization;

[72]   You could probably make the case in
        such a way as to implicate more than
        one person;

[73] You could **again** make sure **that** everyone is in their place, but to do **that** you'd have to turn round all of a sudden;

[74] You could go any time or come any time so as to make sure **that** everyone is in their place;

[75] You could say something in passing, or you could say nothing at all;

[76]   You could tell everything you knew in
        one breath, but the sense of what you
        said would be confined to the breath;

[77]   You could move closer up so as to
        hear what they were saying;

[78]   You could suddenly hear what you'd
        known all along;

[79]   You could find out everything you
        needed to know without asking any
        questions;

[80]   You could, incidentally, even without
        knowing what they were talking about,
        feel drunk with a sense of emotional
        kinship;

[81] You could imagine anyone in any situation, and that would be a comical novelty;

[82] You could, without running the risk of looking silly, suppose that your voice would still be heard — that, too, is a comical novelty;

[83] You could scorn your own system of postulates in an artistic way if your scorn were capable of becoming a comical novelty;

●③⑤

[84]   You could even ignore whatever we can't
       consider a comical novelty;

[85]   You could just not move, literally
       and figuratively, since this, too,
       will pass for a comical novelty;

[86]   You could, in the end, take a little
       bit of everything at random and in
       random amounts — it's no secret that
       this would be a comical novelty;

[87]   You could cultivate your sense of the
       comical to the point that any one of
       the sleepers might suddenly wake up a
       supercomedian;

[88]   You could explain all this all sorts
       of ways;

[89]   You could explain it, for instance,
       as the fear of making a false move;

[90]   You could simply mistake the faint
       glimmers of conceptual outlines for a
       recurrence of the most unbridled
       lyricism of times gone by;

[91] You could think that any conscious
      form is conservative and start with
      that in any assessment of things;

[92] You could think that however it began
      that's how it will end;

[93] You could think that something highly
      unusual is going on;

[94] You could think that nothing happened;

[95] You could just not notice anything;

[96]   You could know already what will end
        how, but to publicize this knowledge
        would not be comical in the least;

[97]   You could declare nebulousness itself
        a constructive principle;

[98]   You could not resist the innate craving
        for leisure and indolence;

[99]   You could perfectly well make do with
        the leftovers from the party, but who
        needs it;

[100] You could search for a nod of genuine
       salvation in fruitless manipulations
       of memory;

[101] You could see the secret sign of a
       fatal torpor in the very fact of
       comical prejudice;

[102] You could avoid a fatal torpor by
       mastering the principles of comical-
       ness once and for all;

[103] You could, on the other hand, refuse to enter into the comical-novelty spirit, but then there's nothing you can do;

[104] You could not accept the given possibilities and decide that nothing happened;

[105] You could continue in the same spirit;

[106] You could stop all this any time — that's one of the virtues of comical novelties;

[107] You could wait for a while, then begin with new energy;

[108]   You could repeat everything from the
        beginning;

[109]   You could not think about the
        consequences: they will naturally be
        comical;

[110]   You could not worry about the future:
        it will naturally be comical.

lev rubinstein

From Beginning
С начала
to End
и до конца

lev rubinstein

[1]   From the very beginning, the usual
        way. But at the same time as if nothing
        had happened before this and nothing
        will happen afterwards.

[2]   Roughly the same way. But at the same
        time as if everything had only just
        begun.

[3]   Approximately the same way. But so
        that the sense of the first impulse
        isn't lost for even a split second.

lev rubinstein

[4]   In the same spirit. But in such a way
      that the sense of freshness and newness
      isn't diminished for even a moment.

[5]   Everything the same way. But at the
      same time so that the feeling of
      confidence keeps growing.

[6]   The same as before. And at the same
      time so that it's entirely obvious
      that everything is all right, that
      everything is in its proper place.

[7] The same as before. And at the same
time banking on the fact that there
won't be any idea of trying to change
the existing situation.

[8] The same way. But so that the existing
situation is imagined to be the only
one possible.

[9] Exactly the same way. But so that a
sense of peace is present the entire
time.

[10] The same way. But so that added to
the sense of permanent peace there is
also a feeling of quiet joy.

lev rubinstein

[11]   The same way. But so that questions
       concerning the future that haven't
       come up yet disappear on their own.

[12]   The same way. But so that any
       recommendations concerning the future
       aren't even considered.

[13]   The same way. But so that the doubts
       that occasionally arise either resolve
       themselves on their own or are rejected
       out of hand as farfetched.

[14]   The same way. But so that there's no
       room for any doubt whatsoever.

[15]   According to the same principle, only
       more so. And so that the constant
       fixation of positive states doesn't
       lead in any way to negative results.

[16]   And so on until the very end. But so
       that there remains the uneasy sense
       that there is also still a real
       possibility of something else.

lev rubinstein

An Elegy
Элегия

lev rubinstein

[1]   Sometimes you ask yourself: "Could
        things be some other way?" And at the
        time, it seems that they probably
        could.

[2]   Sometimes it seems: "This will never
        end!" And there really is no end in
        sight.

[3]   Sometimes you wonder if it's worth
        inhibiting a natural process. And,
        indeed, is it worth it?

5

lev rubinstein

[4] Sometimes it's not at all a bad idea
     to point out the fact that something
     is going on nevertheless;

[5] Sometimes it is appropriate to note
     that as of this time things have shaped
     up to the point that what you might
     call a picture is emerging;

[6] Sometimes a quick glance is enough to
     understand, if not everything, then
     at least the gist.

[7]   Sometimes you think: "What should I
       do now? Should I take full respons-
       ibility for what's happened? Maybe I
       should. But then what?"

[8]   Sometimes you feel that there's
       something about it that both appeals
       to you and repels you at the same
       time.

[9]   Sometimes you suddenly want to look
       inside and, when you do, you wish you
       hadn't.

lev rubinstein

[10]   Sometimes you have such a strange
         thought that afterwards you're
         literally not yourself.

[11]   Sometimes you have such a strange dream
         that, no matter how you look at it,
         it all adds up to the same thing.

[12]   Sometimes you're haunted by ghosts
         and you can't seem to get rid of them...

[13] Sometimes you think about anything at all except what you really need to think about.

[14] Sometimes it suddenly dawns on you that you'll only get what you deserve and that then everything will fall into place.

[15] Sometimes you have the feeling that any day now it will all be settled. Then you remember and you think: "Well, well, well..."

[16] Sometimes you get the feeling that it can't be any other way.

[17]   Sometimes you imagine what it would be like if everything were otherwise, and you think to yourself: "Oh, don't be ridiculous!" — and give it up.

[18]   Sometimes you lie awake all night thinking about the chances you didn't take and don't even see the dawn coming.

[19]   Sometimes you wonder where the confidence that somehow it will all work out comes from.

[20] Sometimes you find yourself listening unwittingly to the muffled voices coming through the wall and realize that they're probably not saying anything very interesting and yet you listen all the harder — my goodness!

[21] Sometimes you go up to a group of people having an animated discussion, hear what they're talking about and just walk away.

[22] Sometimes someone will walk by, say something over his shoulder and disappear, and whether you attach any importance to this or not doesn't really matter.

lev rubinstein

[23] Sometimes you suddenly react violently to something that another time you wouldn't even have noticed.

[24] Sometimes you suddenly realize that you can't even make it to the middle, much less the end. It's too bad, of course...

[25] Sometimes you have the crazy thought: "Well, maybe I should say it out loud?"

[26] Sometimes you're waiting for the right moment to say it, but the moment never comes.

[27]   Sometimes you think to yourself: "Hey, man, why can't you just say it straight? But that's just it. Because, fuckit, 'art', 'art'..."

[28]   Sometimes when someone gets something wrong, it's appropriate to say: "Well, if that's what he thinks, then that's what he thinks. Do I have to explain everything?"

[29]   Sometimes when a certain person's name comes up in conversation you can feel your face change and worry that someone may have noticed.

lev rubinstein

[30] Sometimes you know you're saying or doing the wrong thing but still you can't stop yourself.

[31] Sometimes you try to be as careful as can be, but it doesn't work.

[32] Sometimes you decide to aim for a higher goal and ignore the little things in life, but somehow it doesn't turn out that way.

[33] Sometimes, when you've managed to rise above your emotions and want to help others still at the affect of theirs, you instead find yourself throwing up your hands over the abyss and unable to say anything.

[34] Sometimes a phrase gets stuck in your head and you can't get it out. Never fear: it may contain the hidden meaning in what is going on right now.

[35] Sometimes you rush all over the place in search of peace and quiet when if you'd only just wait a minute you'd get what you wanted.

[36]   Sometimes you seem to be getting closer to something, but it keeps moving further away.

[37]   Sometimes, as you approach the forbidden line, you think for a minute before stepping over it.

[38]   Sometimes there's literally not a minute to lose, yet we keep dragging our feet.

[39]   ometimes you clearly need to give it
        time, but that only occurs to you
        later.

[40]   Sometimes you stare into the distance
        for a long time trying to make
        something out, trying to recognize
        something.

[41]   Sometimes you peer intently into the
        semidarkness without any hope of
        finding it or any fear of misplacing
        it.

[42]   Sometimes you scream so loud you can't
        hear yourself.

[43]   Sometimes you look and look all around
        you and doubt the reality of what is
        going on. But that's not right, though
        it is tempting.

[44]   Sometimes you think and think and in
        the end some sensible solution occurs
        to you.

[45]   Sometimes you wait and wait and nothing
       happens, and then, all of a sudden,
       something goes and happens.

[46]   Sometimes you imagine that the hazel
       branch is a sign of what can never
       be, that the never-ending rain is a
       sign of what will be, and that the
       veiled light in a strange window is a
       sign of the inscrutability of the way.

[47]   Sometimes you sigh and think to
       yourself. And then you sigh again.

lev rubinstein

First It's This,
То одно,
Then It's That
то другое

6 5

lev rubinstein

[1]   First it's this.
       Then it's that.
       Then that.
       And then it's something else again...

[2]   First it's too specific.
       Then it's overly general.
       Then it's neither this nor that.
       And then they start looking over your
       shoulder...

[3]   First it's too wordy.
       Then it's overly terse.
       Then it's just not right.
       And then they tell you to go see...

lev rubinstein

[4] First it's overly vivid.
     Then it's too gloomy.
     Then it's somehow off.
     And then they say you've got to make
     it fit the...

[5] First you can't move.
     Then you can't stop rushing around.
     Then your shoes need a shine.
     And then they start arguing and talking
     such...

[6] First you can't even get past the
     table of contents.
     Then you just have to put up with it.
     Then you get a paper cut.
     And then they all come down on you at
     once...

first it's this, then it's that [1-6]

[7]   First you forget what you were thinking
about all morning.
Then you can't resist some dumb rhyme
like:
"No use looking between his lines,
Only his cock is on his mind."
Then someone goes home sick.
And then you lose your confidence...

[8]   First you're annoyed by the sequence
of your own ideas.
Then your personal experience seems
suddenly worthless.
Then crows start screaming over the
deserted fields.
And then you make the mistake of
looking in the mirror...

[9]   First a chance memory makes your heart
ache.
Then everything around you is covered
with ashes.
Then they hide it so well you'll never
find it.
And then you can't believe what's going
on over there...

lev rubinstein

[10] First your own silence weighs you down.
Then you feel as if you've said
everything you have to say for years
to come.
Then you forget about the inexpressible
beauty of the moment.
And then there's the general uncer-
tainty...

[11] First you hear a noise in the night
and feel scared.
Then some other strange things happen.
Then you feel like giving up when
you're halfway there.
And then you can't figure anything
out...

[12] First the little ball of mercury rolls
away to its grim fate.
Then this terrible memory keeps coming
back to you.
Then the point of it all keeps eluding
you.
And then nature abhors a vacuum...

[13]   First it's light in the East.
        Then it's dark in the West.
        Then it's the daily routine.
        And then it's the times we live in...

[14]   First you can see for miles.
        Then you can't see a thing.
        Then you feel in a fog.
        And then you have to make sense of it
        all...

[15]   First it's about having a good time
        in spite of everything.
        Then it's about what you understand
        and what you don't.
        Then it's about how to cope when your
        last hope is gone.
        And then you never manage to get
        anything done...

[16]   First it's about enthusiasm flagging
in our ranks.
Then it's about ridding ourselves of
the fatal habit of naming everything.
Then it's about the appropriateness
of precisely that point of view.
And then you have to sit there
wondering what you can and can't do...

[17]   First I feel happy and I don't know
why.
Then I feel worried and I don't know
what about.
Then I don't know what appeals to me.
And then there's all this talk...

[18]   First it's the casual glitter of gold.
Then it's a screen with a crack down
it.
Then they say something without
thinking.
And then you have to sit there waiting
for them to address you...

[19]   First it's the fettered flow of
        existence.
        Then it's the meaning in every gesture.
        Then your consciousness begins to
        splinter.
        And then you can't get anyone's
        attention...

[20]   First it's the memory in every crevice
        of the wood.
        Then it's the taste of a love potion.
        Then it's a mix-up in the seating
        arrangement.
        And then they don't want to hear
        anything about it...

[21]   First it's the migratory way of
        eternity.
        Then they're waiting right outside
        the door.
        Then it's the monumental effort it
        takes to focus.
        And then the unseeable suddenly
        presents itself...

lev rubinstein

[22]   First it's memory's drooping head.
        Then it's tomorrow's noonday defector.
        Then they're all over you, pinning
        you down.
        And then you have to explain every-
        thing...

[23]   First it's the chill breath of a night
        wind.
        Then it's the earth's bubbles that
        keep coming up in conversation.
        Then you naively count on getting by
        the same way you always have.
        And then there are those...

[24]   First it's the clear precedence of
        one principle over another.
        Then it's a universality of the kind
        that exists only in dreams.
        Then they can't wait to catch you
        contradicting yourself.
        And then there's this utterly puzzling
        reaction...

[25] First it's the itemized description
of an endless list of possibilities.
Then it's the anticipation of events
that are supposed to be out of this
world.
Then we don't either of us know what's
wrong with us.
And then even what happened seems like
it didn't...

[26] First it's a gray morning after a
sleepless night.
Then it's impossible to encompass the
whole of existence.
Then it's an insuperable longing for
things eternal.
And then even what didn't happen seems
like it did...

[27] First it's one more entry in the ledger
of suffering.
Then various things come up and you
don't know what to do with them.
Then you just have to put up with it.
And then there's not enough room even
·to turn around...

[28]   First it's too many things to worry
       about.
       Then it's what you hope for and take
       comfort in.
       Then it's the sky over Austerlitz.
       And then they finally come to a
       decision...

[29]   First it's the sticky new leaves.
       Then you have to compare everything
       to what's after and before.
       Then it becomes perfectly clear that
       this can't go on forever.
       And then there's no end in sight...

●❼❺

lev rubinstein

Thursday Night,
С четверга
Friday Morning*
на пятницу

lev rubinstein

[1]   All night I kept dreaming of the edges
       of existence. But when I woke up, all
       I could remember was something between
       water and dry land, between silence
       and speech, between sleep and waking,
       and I managed to think, "Here it is,
       the aesthetic of the nebulous. Here
       it is again..."

[2]   I dreamed that someone who, I thought,
       had gone out of my life long ago,
       suddenly appeared and looked at me so
       kindly that I woke up, my heart
       pounding...

[3]   I dreamed that I ought to get up and
       go and see if he was asleep. When I
       woke up I couldn't remember who he
       was. Then it came to me...

[4]   I dreamed that I ought to withdraw
      into myself for a while and then I'd
      think of something. When I woke up, I
      thought, "I don't know, I don't
      know..."

[5]   I dreamed that joy truly knows no
      bounds. When I woke up, I thought,
      "That's what you think..."

[6]   I dreamed that a genuine opportunity
      comes along only four times in life.
      When I woke up, I thought that there
      was definitely something to that...

[7]   I dreamed that the main thing is to
      find the most appropriate expression
      of sympathy for one another. Then I
      woke up...

[8]   I dreamed that the idea of a blank
      sheet of paper is a short circuit of
      any consistent aesthetic experience.
      Then I woke up...

[9]   I dreamed that we can start with the
      fact that our sense of self is in
      fact that of characters whom we
      ourselves have created and who function
      in their own time and space. And that
      this sense of self, as a starting
      point, is what draws us together. Then
      I woke up...

[10]   I dreamed of two whole arguments in
        my favor, but of course I couldn't
        remember them...

[11]   I dreamed of a third argument as well.
        But it, too, remained back there, in
        the dream...

[12]   I dreamed of the long-awaited entrance
        of the hero. Though he often looked
        gloomy, he was clearly always ready
        to laugh. I was especially struck by
        his frank and strained relations with
        reality.
            When I woke up, I thought that
        there was nothing to add to that...

[13]   I dreamed of the rare glimmers of
dying hopes. They shed no light and
afforded no warmth, but only smoldered
quietly in the windless depths of my
consciousness.

I had grown so used to these
glimmers that my tired brain barely
registered them: when they appeared,
my head no longer jerked up, my

nostrils did not flare, my pulse did
not quicken. Nothing, it seemed, could
disturb my dismal calm. Nothing, it
seemed, presaged any change...

[14]   I dreamed of an ancient park, its
trees all lost in thought. Down a
shady alley, a lonely figure was coming
toward me. I had noticed the figure
in the distance and guessed almost
immediately who it was. You've probably
guessed, too...

[15]   I dreamed that they were obviously
not there alone. Someone was stealing
up on them noiselessly in the night,
like a thief. "Quiet," Genrikh mouthed
the word. "Do you hear something?"
They both listened. Again it was quiet.
Then suddenly, like a flash of lightning
tearing through the darkness...

[16]   I dreamed of the creaky floorboards
and balding rugs of a small boarding-
house on the edge of Lake Constance.
The weather during that time was rainy
and unpleasant. The proprietress was
a kind-hearted, roly-poly woman of
maybe fifty. There were generally ten
to twelve guests at meals. All of
different nationalities, habits and

interests. There was absolutely nothing
to talk about, and the dinners had no
savor. Boredom and despondency reigned
at the table.
   One guest, though, did divert my
attention. He was a young, sickly-
looking Italian who never said anything
and only cast occasional, strange,
vague glances as though something he

●❽❸

alone could see had brought him
momentarily out of his habitual
stupor...

[17]   I dreamed of the massive gray edifice
that was the steam-navigation
building. It was a stone's throw from
the apartment where I then lived. My
windows gave on the same dreary square.
And past my windows, morning and
evening, faceless clerks filed. Could
I have imagined then...

[18]   I dreamed of little Kolya's inexpli-
cably happy face, of the intent faces
of relatives, the driver's impatient
face, and all the rest — dear, familiar,
barely familiar and utterly unfamiliar
faces. They all became blurred in
Konstantin's hazy consciousness and
ran together in one wildly spinning
spot while he, as if he'd been shot,

lev rubinstein

collapsed onto the damp morning
pavement of an empty station platform...

[19]   I dreamed that the situation was such
        that even if a pure and trembling
        voice had suddenly risen up amidst
        the inarticulate din, it too would
        have been lost in the gnashing. And
        the few who had managed to hear it
        would merely have exchanged glances
        and nodded knowingly, and that would
        have been the end of it, if not for...

[20]   I dreamed that we all have to feel our
        way in life: here there's a loophole,
        there a fence, there a brick wall. And
        so our lives go by — from decisions to
        doubts, from nods to interjections,
        from dreams to drudgery...

●❽❺

[21]   I dreamed that a light had gone out somewhere there, in the middle. That now you couldn't hear the voice crying in the wilderness. That the warmth had dissipated and could never be recaptured. Only the glance of glass in glass — fleeting and inarticulate...

[22]   I dreamed of acrid smoke and my own death mask. What will we give people to remember us by? What will we take with us? Grace is not for the asking and we do not go in pairs. This is so elementary it doesn't bear explaining...

[23]   I dreamed that my heart was drawn from its sheath in the night. What do we know? What can we do? Let he who knows hold his piece...

[24] I dreamed of the emptiness of the sky. And you and I, we both lost ourselves in it. You said, "That swallow over there will remember us until death."

[25] I dreamed that we would part on the bridge... We were tired, we would rest... Nature has its reasons... We can't very well count on an enthusiastic reception... We neither of us know what tomorrow will bring, let alone the day after... Our last meeting... We'll part on the bridge...

[26] I dreamed that he was lying in the damp earth and not himself. And that the flame of the candle leapt up in the heat of the moment...

[27] I dreamed that he had lain down in
the sand forever. Who understood better
than he the earthly hurly-burly. That
everything is not the way it is...
That the message is always garbled...
      And now our dear friend is looking
down on us...
      We too will go to that place where
water will not flow. Where minds

crumble and screams come out of the
pitch-dark... We too will go: our end
draws nigh; 'tis time that we were
gone. We thought we'd go right on
living and now look what's happened...

[28] At dawn I dreamed of a balcony swathed
in snow, awash in something red, of
the fang-mangled withers of my murdered
stallion, of the fading of little neon
fish instead of the mad-eyed wolves
racing for the woods.
      I heard the rebounding report of a
rifle at my shoulder; an insane giggle

instead of the yelp of a wounded beast...

My dying horse, white steam from the wide-open door, the continuing blizzard, a ski-track overgrown with snow...

[29] I dreamed that my barely breathing ship was going down, while in the raging vastness I composed a marvelous prayer...

[30] I dreamed of two insignificant things: numbness and patience. For now we'll tuck our beaks into our feathers at the intersection of the drafts. We know the true value of that, and the true value of this. But to whom shall we leave the stage when we take up our staff and our beggar's sack? And

how are we to make our way in this
mist, not just for an hour or a day,
but for a thousand years — furiously
thumbing our noses at the world behind
its back, alone with the cold wind?

[31]   I dreamed that they — my remaining
days — were looming up and running
ahead, leaving me behind.
      The flutter of six transparent
wings revealed much to me about myself,
and I woke up...

[32]   I dreamed that he was here, sitting
on the edge of my bed. But it was
clear that he really was here and yet
not here.
      Who knew better than he that
everything was no longer the way it
was before, that there is no refuge
for hope and the unprejudiced mind.

The flutter of six transparent wings revealed much to me about myself, and I woke up...

[33] I dreamed come morning of a half-demon-half-corpse with many eyes in a gilt frame. He said: "It's not worth waiting: a miracle won't happen. If you have somewhere to run, get out of here." He said: "Come with me. I'll show you the way." Then I woke up, my head aching...

[34] I dreamed of the equanimity of paper and of memory nodding off to sleep. To the accompaniment of the routine moisture, I missed yet another spring. A definition of the meaning of existence was on the tip of my tingling tongue. But then a long ray of light fell across my blanket, and I woke up...

[35] I dreamed that sleep brings relief, but that it also takes something away forever. Then I woke up...

[36] I dreamed of the expression "a so-called muse." When I woke up, I lay there for a long time with my eyes open...

[37] I dreamed that telling people dreams you didn't remember was also something to do. When I woke up, I thought, "Why not?"

[38] I dreamed that it doesn't matter who cries over which onion. When I woke up, I thought that, indeed, it doesn't matter...

[39] I dreamed that if they say, "Today is Thursday" on a Thursday, then that means that today is truly Thursday. But if they say, "Today is Thursday" on a Friday, then it's either a lie, or an error, or something else again... When I woke up, I thought that, indeed, it's not only what they say

that's important, but when they say it...

[40]   I dreamed that we were sitting here
        and doing the same thing we are now.
        When I woke up, I thought that there
        was nothing so very unusual about
        that...

[41]   I dreamed of innumerable other
        possibilities and scenarios.
            When I woke up, I spent a long
        time trying to remember at least
        something...
            And just on the edge of sleep and
        waking I dreamed that what is is.
            When I woke up, I thought, "That's
        right..."

---

*According to Russian superstition, the dreams
you dream overnight Thursday are often
prophetic. (*Tr.*)

Communal Fiction
Коммунальное чтиво

lev rubinstein

They say that when in 1918 the first Soviet government moved the capital back to Moscow, and vast hordes of all sorts of people shoved in after them, the so-called housing question became acute. One of those Soviet-People's-Commissar jokers came up with the wonderful idea of "consolidation" and submitted it to the Old Man for his consideration. The Old Man thought about it, but not for long. With his famous squint, he soon said "pensively": "You know, old fellow, I myself am a man of rather old-fashioned habits. I would not, I suspect, be able to live in one apartment with other families. But our comrades? Well, let them try." So his comrades tried. And are still trying to this day.

A communal apartment is not only a space for real (or semi-real, as it begins to seem in retrospect) habitation by real people, but also a permanently operating model of something.

A communal apartment (or *kommunalka*) doesn't measure up to a model village since there isn't even a whiff of the celebrated "community" spirit. A kommunalka reeks of many things, but not of community.

More like villages are the five-story, cement-block buildings put up in places where real villages existed only literally five minutes ago. They are where, it seems to me, the memorable "new collectiveness of people", a thing that is hard to describe but readily understood, finally took shape.

The everyday, formative, ethnic and, if you will, class multivalence of the communal apartment makes it sooner similar to a medieval town.

The same overcrowding.

The same regimentation.

There's even a market square — the kitchen — where goods and information are exchanged: you can borrow an onion until tomorrow or three rubles until your next advance. Or: "Vera Sergeyevna, what do you put in your borshch to make it so rich?"

And a cathedral square: also the kitchen. The role of the cathedral is performed by the relentless kitchen loudspeaker through which citizens are connected to absolute truth and everlasting grace.

The eternally dripping water faucet doubles

as the town fountain. The scenes that take place by the fountain deserve to be written about.

There is a main street: the common corridor. Zigzagging down the corridor overhead are clotheslines trailing socks and long johns.

The neighborly brawls in the kitchen are entirely comparable to the jousting tournaments between knights.

The role of the shady, slightly illusory wood to which the romantic hero of literature flees in moments of despair to weep and to dream is played by the yard. You can dream and weep (especially if you're a sensitive adolescent on the edge of sexual maturity) between the shed and the rusty garage where a trophy motorcycle is rotting along with its sidecar. The motorcycle belongs to Uncle Kolya, a war invalid and accordion player. Uncle Kolya the accordion player doesn't use the motorcycle not only owing to the lack of a complete set of limbs, but on account of the missing motor, sold long since for drink.

The space between the shed and the rusty garage is always freshlyshatupon. It's also where kids go to show each other stupid things. But even our romantic hero can find refuge there worthy of his melancholy. Because this is the YARD: another world, other problems.

Communal existence determined communal consciousness. Communal consciousness gave rise

to the communal myth. With time the myth began
to be travestied into folklore, jokes, platitudes,
prose, and pulp fiction. Communal fiction.

The communal apartment was as much of a mystery
to the foreigner as, say, one's local registration
(or *propiska*). Foreigners either didn't believe
these things really existed, or they demonized
them out of all proportion. In the early '70s,
one American asked if it were true that workers
and intellectuals were put together so that the
intellectuals could educate the workers and the
workers could train the intellectuals in the
spirit of collectivism. He also wondered if it
were true that a person who was registered as
living in Leningrad could not go to Moscow without
permission from the police.

Not knowing what to do with a Dane to whom
another Dane had given my number, I took him to
visit a friend of mine. My friend lived in a
kommunalka. As we made our way down the corridor
hung with old skis and children's washtubs, the
Dane looked round him as if he had been taken
unconscious into some equatorial jungle.

While we sat in my friend's room drinking
the whisky the Dane had brought, a neighbor barged
in twice without knocking: Nikolai Nikolaevich,
clad in a woman's dressing gown from under which
herring-colored long johns peeped out

persuasively. "Aleksandr Markovich," he burst
in the first time, "you don't by any chance have
an enema? Oh! You have guests..." The second
time he came for advice: "Aleksandr Markovich,
what do you think I should do with the kittens?
Drown them or suffocate them better?" Such exotic
questions arose, clearly, because my friend was
a doctor.

At some point the Dane went in search of the
facilities, but wound up in the kitchen. The
sheer quantity of creeping, crawling and flying
insects that met his eyes may have evoked
associations with Western abundance or even the
overproduction of capitalist goods, but I fear
it evoked more spontaneous feelings.

He did eventually find the loo and, had he
been able to read Russian, would have been able
to delight in two signs scrawled in a large
child-like hand and pinned to the wall. The first
championed the stylistics of a May Day slogan:
"Comrades! Flush the urine after you!" The second
was more succinct, but also more abstruse: "No
big pieces!"

As a rule, the various signs found in communal
toilets have been the subject of far less study
than the kindred folklore found in public ones.
Which is too bad. I used to remember any number
of these signs, then I began to forget them. I
remember that in someone's water closet there

lev rubinstein

hung a despair-filled notice whose bizarre accent made it twice as expressive: "No priss on froor". I didn't even guess right away that it was Russian. Was it the memory of a communal childhood that dictated to my friend the poet Viktor Koval his fateful witticism: "On your way to the next world, please turn out the light in this one"?

The whole way back to the metro the Dane maintained a deafening silence. Then he suddenly came out with a surprising thought. "It's good that the doctor doesn't avoid people. People can always go to him for help. That's progressive." The Dane had decided that the doctor was a rich man who had elected to live in this less than convenient, but undoubtedly noble, way. I took to calling my friend Albert Schweitzer. As for the Dane, he was, naturally, an ardent leftist and exceedingly grieved by the dissociation and existential loneliness of people in the West.

The population of a communal apartment was a strict demographic unit, violable in special cases, but otherwise stable.
Who lived or, rather, *resided* there? So then...

You have to have a Klavdia Nikolaevna, a lonely old woman from the erstwhile upper classes and a descendant of the apartment's original owners. She occupies only one room, but a room very enticing to children. The room is stuffed

with antique knickknacks and photographs of mustachioed men in engineer or military uniforms. There's also an out-of-tune piano with a small bust of deaf Beethoven who, for some reason, also seems blind.

You have to have a schoolteacher, an old maid who is forever tormenting Lyuska, a girl of just the opposite type of sexual behavior.

You have to have a Jewish family. Granny, born in the city of Homyel, speaks with a strong accent. Papa, a railway engineer, speaks with a slight accent. Mama. A bright dressing gown. Gets along badly with both the strict schoolteacher and that trollop Lyuska. But is nice to the quiet alcoholic Zhenia an ageless man, a lover of Esenin's poetry and, in rare moments of sobriety, a jack-of-all-trades. Children. The boy, Venya, plays the violin, but dreams of triumphs. "Triumphs-shmriumphs," says Granny. "You want to grow up a gangster? So then say so. Triumphs! Asochnvei! Your grandfather did not have any triumphs, but still everybody come to him to ask what to do." The girl, Ira, is studying mathematics, but dreams of the theater. Although, what theater could that be with an arse like hers.

You have to have the family of a retired pilot from the Ukraine. Merry noisy relatives arrive in constant succession and stay for months.

Two sons: a smart one and a dunce. The smart one is always at the library studying for something. The dunce loves pigeons and smokes between the shed and the rusty garage. (See above.)

You have to have a construction worker who's building the metro. No one ever sees him since he works at night and sleeps during the day. Actually, he was seen once, eating. Ringing the top of an enormous enamel bowl of buckwheat porridge were six or even seven cutlets. This entire magnificence was consumed without haste and in complete silence. His wife, a painted tatterdemalion, has an unbearably obnoxious voice. His daughter is a sniveling tattletale with rat-like eyes. They say she went on to become a deputy in the district soviet.

You have to have a widowed Rosentsveig, a former legal adviser and amateur tenor. Now he's a funny old man reading the evening paper with his fly invariably undone. The teakettle is boiling away which makes for a row: "Yakov Aronich, you'll burn us all to bloody bits!" You can see he's a former philanderer and has "lived". He conducts long telephone conversations with his sister Fira. His tone is slightly irritated. "Fira, let's agree that you can tell me what to do the next time!" He looks meaningfully and helplessly at Tolya the policeman as he walks past.

communal fiction

You have to have a Tolya the policeman. "From Altai myself". His wife, who's also "from somewheres", rules him with an iron hand: she's the jealous type. Apparently not without reason. While shaving in the kitchen before the grease-stained mirror, Tolya passes sentence: "I'm some stud or else the girls've had enough." Otherwise, he's quite good-natured. They either don't have children, or they do, but somehow you don't notice them.

You have to have a Nyurka. She washes dishes in an eatery that serves only dumplings. She has numerous "sweethearts". Some of them don't even make it to Nyurka's room before falling sound asleep in the middle of the corridor. Yakov Aronich, who's in the habit of coming out of his room at night to pee, is always tripping over some silent body. At some point, Nyurka has the d.t.s. It all begins with her cooing and cooing over the three dancing generals on Klavdia Nikolaevna's nickel-plated coffeepot. Nyurka is put in the hospital *for treatment* and Rosentsveig temporarily stops tripping.

You have to have a former NKVD agent with a Baltic last name. Solitary, tight-lipped, gray-haired, in good shape, mysterious. You're afraid of him, naturally. He polishes his boots at length, then goes out to play chess in the local park.

You have to have a wisecracking student named

lev rubinstein

Alik. His parents are away on some permanent assignment. Say, in China: everyone was in China then. Through his door comes the sound of some interminable manutangochachacha. He borrows thirty rubles (old ones) from kind Lyuska. He exasperates the schoolteacher with his Okudzhava. Where he's studying, no one knows. Probably nowhere.

You have to have two sisters: Tatiana and Olga (understandably: *Eugene Onegin*). They are very quiet. They are quiet for a perfectly good reason: they are deaf mutes. But it's only during the day that they're quiet. By night they set about systematically cleaning the places you all use (the corridor, the kitchen, the bathroom, the WC), banging basins and buckets to beat the band. To explain to them that the noise may keep you up, or what noise is, is impossible. So you all just put up with it. For one thing, they're invalids of a sort. For another, they're dressmakers, besides which they're kind. Every tenant receives something on his birthday: wide sateen trousers or an apron with the emblem of the Moscow Youth Festival on it. The festival's playful daisy evokes parasitic associations since it is affixed to the place usually reserved for the fig leaf.

You have to a have a Tatar woman named Saida. She washes the floors at our school. Her son

communal fiction

Rinat is studying to be a ballet dancer at the Bolshoi Theater. He is the legitimate pride of the apartment: he's been shown twice on television at a government concert. In the evening Saida drinks two glasses of Three Sevens, then stumbles into the kitchen and screams: "Rinatik, call a chair!" Impeccable Rinatik "calls a chair", Saida hoists herself up onto it and goes into a long song and dance about something, gradually slipping into her native Tatar. On Tatar holidays, they made these delicious little meat pies. Or maybe it only seems that way to me now, that they were so delicious. Because no one remembers anything exactly the way it was. The novelization of memory? A self-protective device? The patina of time?

And you have to have all the rest except for all the others.

The communal kitchen is a self-sufficient communicative space. There, against the hum of the unceasing radio receiver, an equally unceasing conversation goes on and on, as wildly various thematically as it is stylistically. A conversation about everything. A long Conversation often fraught with the spontaneous actions of its participants.

This Conversation formed the basis of several works by the artist Ilya Kabakov. One of them, a work called *"Olga Georgievna, your kettle is*

lev rubinstein

boiling", is an endless series of entirely discrete and absolutely authentic conversational gestures produced by the communal kitchen's communal body. For instance: *"Vera Yakovlevna, don't pour anything into the garbage pail, that's what makes it smell and spreads germs. Oh, what am I saying? I'm all mixed up. I meant the trashcan. Of course you can pour things into the garbage pail, that's what it's there for, but peelings and paper go in the trash..."*

It's obvious what inspired Kabakov. Climbing the stairs to his studio on the seventh floor of the famous Rossiya building on Sretensky Boulevard, you could hear anything you liked through the doors. "Oh, so you're a lawyer, are you?" I once heard. "You're not a lawyer, you're a little prick! Got that!"

The kommunalka and art is another subject altogether and practically inexhaustible. As soon as communal apartments appeared in life, they appeared in literature. Zoshchenko, Bulgakov, Kharms, Ilf and Petrov, proceeding from different, sometimes fundamentally different, aesthetic premises and pursuing different artistic aims, showed us "vivid models".

The most sensitive writers realized that the communal apartment was a new social organization and, therefore, a new language. Such newborn lexical grotesqueries as *"upravdom"* and *"domkom"*

communal fiction

became firmly entrenched in the literary language, "*consolidated*" it and occupied "*floor space*" in it. The communal apartment, even before the collective farm and the Gulag, was a sign of how rapidly the utopia was mutating into an anti-utopia.

Then came film. Stalin-era movies managed somehow not to notice the communal apartment. The heroes lived in modest but tidy workers' settlements, or in snug log huts, or in vast professorial apartments with glass doors and a view of the Kremlin.

The kommunalkas lived in by funny, slightly nutty graduate students with a habit of leaving their glasses in the most inappropriate places; by warm-hearted, provincial grandmothers bearing plates piled high with freshly baked pies; and by malicious matrons in curlers always listening at the door, appeared in the '60s. And once they'd appeared, they couldn't disappear.

They haven't disappeared to this day. From art, from memory, or from life.

The Hero Appears
Появление героя

[1]   Well what can I tell you?

[2]   He knows, but he's not saying.

[3]   I don't know. Maybe you're right.

[4]   It tastes good and it's good for you.

[5]   By the first car at seven.

[6]   The part about the schoolboy's further
      on.

[7]   I'll show you. It's on my way.

[8]   Well, have you decided anything?

[9]   He got on – and went to the end of the
      line.

lev rubinstein

[10]   Listen to what I wrote.

[11]   Or straight through the yard.

[12]   Has he been a terrible bother?

[13]   Or tomorrow — there's no rush.

[14]   Three times a day before meals.

[15]   Quit fooling around.

[16]   In the notions store on the corner.

[17]   Around a hundred to a hundred and twenty.

[18]   So here's what I have to say.

111

the hero appears [1-18]

[19]   Come on in — I'll be right there.

[20]   Don't give me those pathetic excuses.

[21]   Now, then, stick out your tongue and
        say 'Ahhhhhhh...'

[22]   So, are we going or not?

[23]   That's all right. It's not heavy.

[24]   Oh, come on! Are you serious or are
        you just saying that?

[25]   But you shouldn't do that, you know.

[26]   What — are you completely out of your
        mind?

[27]   Let's try again.

[28] Thank you, I can do it myself.

[29] I don't know, I'm just used to it.

[30] I'm not doing this for my sake!

[31] You're wrong, too, you know.

[32] What does it say about the schoolboy?

[33] I told you: stay out of this!

[34] Leave me alone — I feel awful.

[35] But you should've called and asked...

[36] He always looks so angry and morose...

113

the hero appears [19-36]

[37]   You might at least open a window.

[38]   One more time — then everybody goes
        home.

[39]   The grub there's first class.

---

[40]   I'm just exhausted.

[41]   What rhymes with 'five'?

[42]   Stubborn, like I don't know what.

---

[43]   Six letters. Ends with a P.

[44]   Okay. Bye. I'll call you.

[45]   Him? Maybe fifty. Why?

---

[46]   Did you turn the iron off?

[47]   Just walks in and sits down.

[48]   Have you looked in a mirror lately?

[49]   Oh, come on! There's nothing to feel
        sorry about.

[50]   I should've stayed home.

[51]   So what did you want to ask me?

[52]   I know what I'm talking about.

[53]   Tried it on... and it was just right.

[54]   Just one more time?

[55]   Ask someone else.

[56]   Thank you, no. I really must go.

[57]   And you, like a fool, believed that?

[58]   He's plastered before breakfast.

[59]   Why don't you go outside and play
       with Mitya.

[60]   Does she know whose it is?

[61]   He'll be a year next week.

[62]   You're kidding? I didn't know that.

[63]   Now, are you finished? Can I say
       something?

[64]   I don't care one way or the other.

[65]   What do you say we walk to the metro?

[66]   Sleeps till one every day, the bum.

[67]   And he's not a good speller.

[68]   Your soul can't die!

[69]   They've started letting them go so
        quickly.

[70]   I'm so thirsty — can't stop drinking.

[71]   He keeps saying his stomach hurts.

[72]   Who's not snoring? You're not snoring?

117

the hero appears [55-72]

[73]   Confucius — is that the fifth century?

[74]   Tell them to oil the bed.

[75]   Can I ask what you're talking about?

[76]   I don't care. You decide.

[77]   Comrades, let's try to keep it short.

[78]   So what should I do, call the police?

[79]   But how can you live like that?

[80]   Did he at least say thank you?

[81]   She's made a complete mess of things!

[82]   Finish talking. I'm expecting a call.

[83]   I feel too embarrassed. You ask.

[84]   You should've just fixed it.

[85]   Oh, sweetie. It's almost over.

[86]   You're just an idiot!

[87]   Twelve? In one night? You must be joking!

[88]   Spit that junk out right now!

[89]   It was brought from abroad.

[90]   Closed for repairs.

[91]   Laundry accepted from twelve to three.

[92]   Can't hear me? I'll call you right
       back.

[93]   But where's the part about the
       schoolboy?

[94]   I didn't say that.

[95]   The schoolboy went to school. When he
       got to school, he went into his
       classroom and sat down at his desk.
       It was drawing class. The schoolboy
       drew a teacup in his sketchbook. The
       teacher said it was a good drawing
       and he praised the schoolboy for his
       drawing. Then the bell rang and the
       schoolchildren went to recess. The

120

lev rubinstein

schoolboy was alone in the classroom
and he began to think.

[96] The schoolboy invited other children
from his class to his birthday party:
two girls and three boys. They had
seven pieces of sponge cake to eat
and five bottles of Baikal to drink.
One girl ate two pieces of cake and
drank a bottle and a half of the
Baikal. One of the three boys drank
the rest of the Baikal on a bet and

said that he could have drunk more.
They didn't finish the cake: there
was one whole piece left over and one
with a bite taken out of it. After
the cake and the Baikal, the children
played guessing games. The birthday
was very interesting and lots of fun.
When the guests were gone, the schoolboy was alone and he began to think.

[97] The schoolboy bought some copybooks at the store. Four of them were lined and the rest were checked. When he got home, the schoolboy stacked the new copybooks neatly on the table. Then the schoolboy sat down at the table and began to think.

[98] The schoolboy's mother gave him one ruble and told him to go to the store and buy two 16-kopek cartons of milk and a loaf of Riga bread. (If there was any. If there wasn't, then half a loaf of any black bread, whatever was freshest.) The schoolboy did what his mother told him. He bought two cartons of milk and half a loaf of Borodino

bread. (There wasn't any Riga.) When he got home, the schoolboy gave his mother the milk and the bread and the change, but not all: his mother let him keep the copper coins. Then he sat down by the window and began to think.

[99] The schoolboy asked the teacher: "May I be excused? My head really aches." The teacher said: "You may go. Your head seems to ache an awful lot." The schoolboy went away and began to think.

[100] The schoolboy asked: "Whether you dissolve into existence or dissolve into non-existence — isn't it all the same?" The teacher said: "I don't know." The schoolboy went away and began to think.

[101] The teacher asked: "Have you read 'Songs of the Zhou Kingdom' and 'Songs of the Chao Kingdom'?" The schoolboy replied: "No." The teacher said: "Anyone who hasn't read these is like someone standing with his face to the wall in silence." The schoolboy didn't say anything. He went on his way and began to think.

❶❷❸

the hero appears [97-101]

[102]   The teacher said: "I don't want to say anything more." The schoolboy said: "If the teacher doesn't want to say anything more, then what will we have to pass on?" The teacher said: "Have you ever heard the sky say anything? But still the seasons come and go, and things are born." The schoolboy went away and began to think.

[103]   At first he thought: "Where can I look? Because on all sides of me — in front and in back, to the right and to the left, above and below, in breadth and in depth — I see nothing but the confused expanse of our arrhythmic efforts and claims. So where can I look?"

[104]   Then he thought: "The circle has been drawn and there's nowhere... But if you think hard, then you'll find the only possible solution while at the same time other voices keep insisting that you're not alone..."

[105]   Then he thought: "Joy goes home without having recognized any of us while at the same time something keeps calling itself to mind..."

[106]   Then he thought: "Hark! The wind is playing such a trick with the treetops that they won't soon recover, while at the same time it's becoming clearer and clearer that if you stop, you won't be able to pick up all the pieces..."

[107]   Then he thought: "As we edge closer to the forbidden line, will we gain something from each other, while at the same time the seasons contract and expand and you no longer know what's when..."

[108]   Then he thought: "As we edge closer
         and closer to the indisputable limit,
         it's time, it seems, that we come to
         our senses, while at the same time
         the causes and effects keep changing
         places and you no longer know what's
         where..."

[109]   Then he thought: "As we edge closer
         and closer to the boundary described,
         what if we suddenly don't have enough
         strength, while at the same time I'm
         trying to grasp the threads of either
         thoughts or memories that are slipping
         away and I cannot, I cannot, I can-
         not..."

[110]   Then he thought for a long time.

'The Cat Wore a Hat'
Мама мыла раму

[1]   The cat wore a hat.

[2]   Papa bought a television.

[3]   The wind blew.

[4]   Zoya was stung by a wasp.

[5]   Sasha Smirnov broke his leg.

[6]   Borya Nikitin was hit in the head
       with a stone.

[7]   It rained.

[8]   His brother teased him.

[9]   The milk boiled over.

128

lev rubinstein

[10] His first word was "collarbone".

[11] Yura Stepanov made a teepee.

[12] Yulia Mikhailovna was strict.

[13] Vova Avdeyev was a bully.

[14] Tanya Chirkova was stupid.

[15] Galya Fomina's fiance had only one
      arm.

[16] Sergei Aleksandrovich had his own
      telephone put in.

[17] The invalid burned to death in the
      car.

[18] We went walking in the forest.

[19] Granny had cancer.

[20] Granny died in her sleep.

[21] I often dreamed about Granny.

[22] I was very afraid of dying in my sleep.

[23] Igor Dudkin looked Georgian.

[24] Sergei Aleksandrovich joked with Papa.

[25] The Sorokins had plum trees, but they also had a dog.

[26] The boys were playing volleyball in the field.

lev rubinstein

[27] Gleb Vyshinsky brought a mouse to school.

[28] Volodya Voloshenko told lies.

[29] Elena Illarionovna knew the poet Sasha Chorny.

[30] The power kept going down.

[31] There was an interesting movie on at the cinema.

[32] His brother turned on the record player.

[33] Papa had a fit.

[34] The dog Buyan was rattling his chain.

[35] Sasha Smirnov envied my stamps.

[36]   He could wiggle his ears.

[37]   Then I learned how.

[38]   Polina Mironovna said that her son's
        a dolt.

[39]   Klavdia Efimovna's husband's name was
        Mikhail Borisovich.

[40]   Raisa Savelyevna worked at Gastronome
        No. 40 as an economist.

[41]   Yurka Vinnikov was her son.

[42]   Ksenia Alekseyevna was not bright,
        but she was very kind.

[43]   The Aronovs, Pavlik and Rita, lived
        in the next building.

[44]   Tanya Chirkova, by the way, also lived
        in that building.

[45]   Unfortunately, I can't remember the
        name of Raika Guseva's husband.

[46]   The wind blew.

[47]   My brother told me what Mama and Papa
        were doing in the next room.

[48]   We also grew sorrel, radishes and
        leeks.

[49]   Slava Novozhilov had a scar from a
        wire hockey stick.

[50]   It rained.

[51]   I was afraid of Tanya Beletskaya's
        dolls.

[52] Yura Stepanov's father didn't have any teeth, his mother was fat, and his sister was kooky.

[53] His sister's name was Yulia.

[54] I didn't have a sister, but I had a brother.

[55] My brother said that Stalin died today.

[56] My brother punched me because I laughed and made faces.

[57] Papa quit smoking.

[58] We hoped there'd be a war soon.

[59] We liked the Chinese.

[60] I wasn't allowed to cross the street.

[61] Once I nearly suffocated to death.

[62] Galya Fomina was studying at a teacher's college. When I asked her why it was raining, she began to explain: "In our country there are many bodies of water..." I didn't understand the rest or remember it.

[63] Sasha Smirnov had a habit of farting inside.

[64] There wasn't any sound, but it stank.

[65] He never admitted he did it.

[66]   I learned to ride a bicycle.

[67]   I was embarrassed to tell anyone my
       name.

[68]   Once I saw such an enormous caterpillar,
       I never forgot it.

[69]   I was often sick to my stomach.

[70]   Once I went into Galya Fomina's room
       without knocking and saw it for the
       first time.

[71]   Once, seized by terrible misgivings,
       I rushed straight in.

[72]   They came, but very late.

lev rubinstein

[73]   The wind roared all night and there
        was also thunder and lightning.

[74]   It was terrible weather, everything
        was in flux and flowing.

[75]   A wind began to blow from around the
        corner and the air turned raw and
        sad.

[76]   Thunder struck, tedium came up, and
        panic surged in my breast.

[77]   In the darkness it whistled and it
        glittered, hail hammered hard on the
        roof.

[78]   The tops of the fir trees trembled,
        black clouds hung over the porch.

[79]   The beginning was like all beginnings,
        but it all ended with a bang.

[80]   Above me everything was as before,
        but below me the ground rocked.

[81]   We careened, collapsed and flailed,
        then went our separate ways.

[82]   That day everything was the way it
        always was.

[83]   I got up, got dressed...

The Smoke of the
ДЫМ ОТЕЧЕСТВА,
Fatherland,
or a Filter Gulag
ИЛИ ГУЛАГ С ФИЛЬТРОМ

lev rubinstein

These days in Moscow cigarettes are advertised in the most resplendent fashion on enormous outdoor billboards at the bottom of which — according to the law of the genre — we are reminded, in fine and unconvincing print, that, actually, smoking isn't all that good for our health. In other words, the attractive, happy and even excessively healthy people in the outsize posters can puff away with impunity. But for people like you and me, smoking is apparently dangerous. I don't believe it! The Health Ministry's pitiful prattle about the hazards of smoking against the background of the ads' triumphant bacchanalia carries no more weight than does the formulaic civility in a verbal construction like: "Excuse me for saying so, but you are a horse's ass!" But that's just by the way. Especially as non-smokers don't need any convincing, while confirmed smokers don't need any ads. They particularly didn't need any ads

lev rubinstein

not long ago when crazed consumers of "the smoke of the Fatherland" took to turning empty cigarette stands upside down.

Filter cigarettes made their debut in the early '60s. Domestic ones included. Or rather, domestic ones specifically. The first, it seems, were Krasnopresnenskiye; the second, Novost. Or maybe it was the other way round, I don't remember. Side by side with hip cafes, jazz and abstract art, filter cigarettes — as opposed to totalitarian, Stalinist *papirosi* — became signs of the thaw and of liberalism in general. It is difficult to convey the sweet feeling of initiation into world civilization with which one slowly undid the little red cellophane strip, with which one put the glossy pack on the plastic cafe tabletop for all the world to see, and with what Hemingway-and-Aksyonovesque abstraction one exhaled the smoke through one's nose. "Old man, would you have a cigarette on you?" That's a far cry from: "Hey kid, gotta papiroska?" That's culture. The West, freedom, progress, glass and concrete, outer space, *Yunost* magazine, polymers and pointy moccasins for fifteen rubles a pair. The coming of the filter-cigarette age divided the smoking community into the up-to-date and the old-regime, into modernists and fundamentalists, into Westernizers and patriots.

The pre-filter and essentially *papirosi*

141

civilization wasn't homogeneous either. One or
another preference said more about a person than
the preferences themselves. Stalin, as portrayed
in hundreds of movies and novels, stuffed his
pipe with tabacco from Gertsegovina Flor *papirosi*.
The gray-at-the-temples prison warden usually
uttered his sacramental "the Tambov wolf is your
comrade now"* between two puffs of a Kazbek. The
big boys behind the shed smoked cheap Severs. In
the folklore of young smokers, Sever somehow
rhymed with *treepper* (gonorrhea). As in: "Anyone
who smokes Sever is sure to get *treepper*." What
nonsense. Even children knew that smoking
something even as vile as Sever was fraught with
all sorts of things, but not that. Then again,
poetry is beyond truth, isn't that true?

The most democratic and most statistically
average thing to smoke was Belomors. At first,
everyone smoked them. Then, in the filter era,
the most stubborn. Later, and evidently to this
day, aging human rights activists as a symbol of
their ascetism. The most portentous aspect of a
Belomor is its name, which has survived
everything. Imagine a German cigarette called
Auschwitz or Buchenwald. Consider as well the
smoking chimneys and the similarity becomes
ridiculous. You could split your sides laughing.
Only why go butting into German history when we
have our own just as good. The name Belomorkanal

is not, in essence, very different from the name Gulag.

What has prompted the remarks above and below is the recent appearance in cigarette kiosks of an amazing mutant: a Belomor cigarette with a filter. The similar Prima appeared a little earlier. But in a socio-cultural context, a Prima as against a Belomor is like a carpenter as against a cabinetmaker. So then, a filter Belomor. With the same sickeningly familiar picture on the pack. A new wine in an old wineskin. The appearance of this remake evokes a bright bundle of meaningful metaphors. That this gimmick belongs to the "old-songs-about-the-main-thing"** class is clear. Perhaps even too clear. What isn't associated today with those ill-fated "songs"? This hackneyed formula seems to have enveloped our entire time and space symbolically. In other words, our space is going through a time of "old songs" — our own inevitably specific and local recension of postmodernism. It's as if to say we had a great era once. And now that great era has been fitted with a filter. So that you cough less. Cough less blood, too.

Meanwhile, the new and improved Belomor is this: typical socialism with a human face. Or, to put it a bit more crudely: a filter Gulag. It is, like other large and small features of the "velvet" restoration, the same thing as today's

1 4 3

Stalinist anthem without the Stalinist words: the anthem, too, has been fitted with a kind of filter.

That's really all I have to say.

Oh, I almost forgot: "Smoking, dear reader, is hazardous to your health".

---

*Once imprisoned, the Soviet man forfeited the right to address a superior as "comrade". From now on the proper form of address was "citizen". If the prisoner forgot, and addressed the warden as "comrade", the warden would set him straight: "The Tambov wolf is your comrade now." (*Tr.*)

**Old Songs About the Main Thing is the name of a recent TV program on which singers sang schmaltzy old Soviet songs that were especially popular twenty, thirty and forty years ago. The program became a symbol of nostalgia for the Soviet era. (*Tr.*)

That's Me

ЭТО Я

[1]   That's me.

[2]   That's me, too.

[3]   And that's me.

[4]   That's my parents. In Kislovodsk, I
      think. The inscription says: "I952".

[5]   Misha with his volleyball.

[6]   Me with my sled.

lev rubinstein

[7]   Galya with two kittens. It says: "Our
      pets' corner".

[8]   I'm third from the left.

[9]   The market in Ufa. It says: "Market
      in Ufa. I940".

[10] I don't know what that is. It says:
      "For dear Yolochka, to remember me
      by, from M.V., city of Kharkov".

[11]   That's my father in his pajamas holding
       a mattock. It says: "Working hard."
       The handwriting is mine.

[12]   Mama with the deaf dressmaker Tatiana.
       Both in bathing suits. It says: "It's
       hot. Summer '54".

[13]   That's me in underpants and an
       undershirt.

[14]   Seated:

[15]   Felix Lazutin.

[16]   *(Someone's hand writing something on a sheet of paper.)*

[17]   Arkady Lvovich Golubovsky.

[18]   *(A drop of rain slipping down the window of a train car.)*

[19]   Rosalia Leonidovna.

[20]   *(A small pink envelope that has fallen*
        out of a woman's purse.)

[21]   Alevtina Nikitichna Koshelyova, a
        cleaning woman.

[22]   *(The soundlessly moving lips of a*
        television announcer.)

[23]   The late A.V. Sutyagin.

[24]   *(Part of a photograph floating down a*
        spring rivulet.)

lev rubinstein

[25]   A.P. Gavrilin. At school they called
        him "Taxidermist".

[26]   *(The distended veins on the arms of
        an elderly worker.)*

[27]   Prof. Witte.

[28]   *(An open umbrella floating slowly out
        from under a bridge.)*

[29]   Standing:

[30]   I.S. Martemianov.

[31]　Now we see a solitary leaf desperately
　　　resisting an icy fall wind.

[32]　And it says: "What do I have to do
　　　with it?"

[33]　S.Ya. Mogilevskaya and V.N. Pilipenko.

[34]　Now we see ringlets of golden hair
　　　cascading to the floor.

[35]　And it says: "Everyone's to blame,
　　　but you have to answer."

[36]   G.Ya. Tolpygin.

[37]   Now we see the tear-stained face of
       an Italian woman, a TV reporter.

[38]   And it says: "Many years have gone by
       since then, and you are still the
       person you were, as the poet whose
       name I can't even remember once said".

[39]   Joachim Sartorius.

[40]   Now we see a jack of spades that's
       been torn in half and left on the
       seat of a leather armchair.

[41]   And it says: "Here we'll have every-
        thing: the plash of an oar and the
        tender words 'I love you' to one not
        yet old enough to make eyes at the
        king".

[42]   T.Kh. Sittova.

[43]   Now we see six or even seven bright
        orange tablets in the palm of a child's
        trembling hand.

[44]   And it says: "That's the person I'll
        be till I die. Otherwise I'll stumble
        and fall. No wonder I was so afraid
        of my mother and always did what she
        said."

[45]   O.A. Makeyeva.

[46]   Now we see the city of Bochum marked
       on a map.

[47]   And it says: "The habit of existing
       like that dates back to the time when
       children weren't allowed to make noise
       or interfere."

[48]   V.N. Konotopov.

[49]   Now we see a small pile of dog shit
       bearing the fresh imprint of a bicycle
       tire.

[50] And it says: "When you're tired of waiting for trouble at home and can't wait anymore, then remember the large black footprints on the freshly washed floor."

[51] V.N. Zamesov.

[52] Here we see a child's hesitant finger picking out the melody of Schubert's *Trout* on the piano.

[53] And it says: "Patience and glory are two sisters, yet neither one knows the other. Be quiet and keep out of sight until you're asked to join the fight."

lev rubinstein

[54] In the semidarkness we make out the silhouette of an enormous rat nuzzling the face of a sleeping child.

[55] That's me.

[56] Here there finally appears the large silver button on the riding-cloak of a young man on his way to visit a dying relative.

[57] A dueling pistol trembling in the hand of a lame officer.

[58] A French novel, opened to the middle, trembling in the hand of a young lady.

[59]   A silver snuffbox trembling in the
        hand of a pale young man.

[60]   A small tin cross trembling in the
        hand of a drunken soldier.

[61]   A large silver samovar trembling in
        the hands of a drunken army surgeon.

[62]   The shiny and slightly trembling beak
        of a big black bird sitting motionless
        on the head of a plaster bust of an
        ancient goddess.

[63] That's all me.

[64] Felix Lazutin: "Thank you, but I have to go."

[65] *(Goes out)*

[66] Martemianov, Igor Stanislavovich. *A Season of Revelations: Coll. Lit.- Crit. Articles.* Moscow: Sovremennik, 1987.

[67]   Arkady Lvovich Golubovsky: "All right
       then. I think I'll be going."

[68]   *(Goes out)*

[69]   Tolpygin, Gennady Yakovlevich.
       Epiphany Sizzles: Verses and Poems.
       Tula: Priokskoye Pub., 1986.

[70]   Rosalia Leonidovna: "It's late. I have
       to go."

[71]   *(Goes out)*

[72]   Mogilevskaya, Susanna Yankelevna;
        Pilipenko, Vladimir Nikolaevich. *We're
        Having Fun! How About You?: Repertory
        Coll. for 4th, 5th and 6th Graders
        with Hearing Loss.* Moscow: Prosvesh-
        cheniye, 1984.

[73]   Alevtina Nikitichna Koshelyova, the
        cleaning woman: "Oh, dear! What'm I
        doin' sittin' here like this? I gotta
        go."

[74]   *(Goes out)*

[75]   Joachim Sartorius. *Decoding the Wheel:
        A Novel.* Tr. from German and postface
        by V.A. Rivkina. Moscow: Nauka, 1984.

[76] The late A.V. Sutyagin: "Lyubochka, do you ever have the feeling that everything that's happening to you and around you — that old woman over there, see her?, looking for something in her bag, or that cat that just ran around the corner — that all this is filled with a great and mysterious meaning which, if you just made a

little effort, you would understand once and for all? I'm sorry, what did you say?"

[77] "Nothing. I'm listening."

[78] "So, do you ever have that feeling or not?"

[79] "What feeling?"

[80] *(Goes out)*

[81] Shittova, Tamara Kharitonovna. *Some Questions Concerning the Unconventional Poetics in the Later Works of James Dawson.* In *Aktualny Labirint* (3rd ed.), Moscow, 1992 (pp. 12-21).

[82] Makeyeva, Olga Aleksandrovna. *Calendrical Rites Among Tribes of the Middle Left Bank.* Ibid, pp. 12-21.

[83] Konotopov, Valery Nikolaevich. *Thomas Bauer's Drama "The Cowgirl and the Kingmaker": An Analysis of the Dominant Motifs.* Ibid, pp.12-21.

[84]   Zamesov, Viktor Nikolaevich. *The Crisis
         of the Parasitogenic Consciousness:
         What's Next.* Ibid, pp. 12-21.

[85]   A.P. Gavrilin: "For example, we say:
         'The wind is making so much noise.'
         Am I right?"

[86]   "Well, yes..."

[87]   "But it's not the wind that's making
         the noise, it's everything in its way:
         the branches on the trees, the sheet
         metal on the roofs, the chimneys. But
         the wind, Lyubochka, doesn't make any
         noise. Why should it?"

[88]   "Indeed..."

[89]   *(Goes out)*

[90]   Prof. Witte *(Alone)*: "Good Lord! How long can this go on? I simply cannot get over it! I mean to say, I am honestly trying. God can see that I am."

[91]   *(Starts shouting)*

[92]   "This is all because of her! Her! That mindless philistine Antonina! And as for what her delightful cousin has cost me, that hateful scoundrel done up in a university diploma, God alone knows. Actually, I think I know what to do!"

[93]   *(Goes out)*

[94] "Now look. First you have to wipe it with this sponge. Look, I'm showing you how. With this sponge. Then with this dry rag. So it doesn't rust. See?"

[95] *(Goes out)*

[96] "They told me they would come by on the holiday, in the evening. So I baked an apple cake. They like apple cake. Then I changed my clothes and sat down to wait. And suddenly they call me from the Schusters and say that the Schusters invited them so they went. How can they do that? I was so upset. Sitting there like a

fool with my cake. I called you because I thought you might come by and have some. You like apple cake, too. But you weren't home either. I even cried a little. I felt so depressed: Well, anyway, doesn't matter now..."

[97] *(Goes out)*

[98]   "You know, I think I'll go."

[99]   "Don't be absurd. You can't go anywhere now! Look, you can have the whole attic to yourself. We have pillows, blankets, everything..."

[100]   "No, no. Thank you. *(Looks at his watch)* Ten past twelve. I can still make it."

[101]   "Well, all right. Good luck."

[102]   *(Goes out)*

[103]   And that's me.

[104]   That's a golden morning with this simple kid who lived next door running away from furious Aunt Zoya.

[105]   And that's me.

lev rubinstein

[106] That's Raya Laricheva's half-forgotten silhouette. My glasses in simple frames. I'm nine, she's twelve.

[107] And that's me.

[108] Those are the four words Sanya said when Kolya bent the horseshoe, then couldn't unbend it.

169

[109]   And that's me.

[110]   Here's festive holiday Moscow, red
         flags flying and cries of "hooray!",
         and girls from our yard, their faces
         freshly washed to honor the day.

[111]   And that's me.

lev rubinstein

[112] That's the lovely sound of the Stalinist anthem at exactly six a.m., as if I'd been up all night. Someone must have forgotten to turn off the radio receiver.

[113] And that's me.

[114] That's me in underpants and an undershirt.

[115] That's me in underpants and an undershirt with my head under the covers.

[116]   That's me in underpants and an
         undershirt with my head under the
         covers running across a sunny glade.

[117]   That's me in underpants and an
         undershirt with my head under the
         covers running across a sunny glade,
         and my marmot with me.

[118]   And my marmot with me.

[119]   *(Goes out)*

172

Here I Am
Я здесь

lev rubinstein

[1]   So then, here I am!

[2]   Well...

[3]   Well, here I am...

[4]   (Where'd you come from? We didn't think
      you'd turn up...)

[5]   Well...

[6]   Well, here I am! I can't tell you the
      feeling...

[7]   ...the sensation...

[8]   ...the feeling...

[9]   (Look at you... so dashing, big and strong, I would hardly have...

[10] ...recognized you.)

[11] So then...

[12] So then, here I am! What could be more wonderful than this magical...

[13] ...What could be more magical...

[14] ...than this wonderful...

175

[15] (And now my headache's gone, it's easier to breathe, and generally...

[16] ...I feel better.)

[17] Well...

[18] Well, here I am! No other place...

[19] ...like it...

[20] It's a place like...

[21] ...no other...

[22] (Now that's much better. Because, to tell you the truth, I was beginning to think that if this was the way it was going to be then we'd better just...

[23] ...forget about it.)

[24] So then...

[25] So then, here I am! I would never have dreamed...

[26] Who would have dreamed...

[27] ...only yesterday...

[28] *(Repeat four times)*

[29]   Well...

[30]   Well, here I am! It's incredible,
        but...

[31]   Hard to believe...

[32]   ...but...

[33]   *(The remains of a sad fire crackle in
        the grate)*

[34]   So then...

[35]   So then, here I am! I won't bore...

[36]   ...I won't bore...

[37]   ...you...

[38]   ...you, the reader...

[39]   Aged 54, works in the planning
       department of a research institute.

[40]   Re-married.

[41]   Has a grown son from her first
       marriage.

[42]   Looks young for her age, in good shape.

[43]   Likes to sing and plays the guitar
       "just for fun."

[44]   Was coming back from her lunch break
       at around 2:30 p.m....

[45]   *(Well...)*

[46]   Aged 39, drives a cab.

[47]   Used to lift weights when he was
       younger, then gave it up.

[48]   Married.

[49]   Two children... Denis, I4, and Lada, 9.

[50] Started his shift at around 2:30 p.m.
and headed for Domodedovo Airport...

[51] *(So then...)*

[52] Aged 24, teaches kindergarten.

[53] Around 5'8" or 5'9".

[54] Pretty, a bit on the heavy side.

[55] Lives with her parents.

[56] Not married but seems to have a steady
boyfriend.

[57]   She was standing at the tram stop
       near Riga Station at around 2:30
       p.m....

[58]   *(Well...)*

[59]   Aged 5I, stage actor.

[60]   Suffered a major heart attack three
       years ago.

[61]   Gets mostly small parts.

❶❽❷

lev rubinstein

[62] He left the theater at around 2:30 p.m., after rehearsal, and decided to walk the couple of stops instead of taking the bus...

[63] *(So then...)*

[64] Basically, the whole thing has to be exceedingly light, almost transparent, barely discernible.

[65] Could be something like a rainbow.

[66] Whereas the description of a house can start anywhere.

[67]   With the color of the roof, say.

[68]   Or with something growing in the
        garden.

[69]   An old white willow by the fence, for
        instance.

[70]   Or something like when you think that
        you're just pretending to be asleep
        but in fact are really sleeping.

[71]   Or like when someone sneaks up on you
        from behind, puts his hands on your
        shoulders and starts laughing in such
        a familiar way you can't keep from
        crying.

[72] Or imagine that you're living in
      constant fear of some **appalling**
      catastrophe.

[73] I think **that's** why you instinctively
      resist any life changes.

[74] "I just can't keep sewing that idiotic
      half-belt back on for you every god-
      damned day!"

[75] *(Throws the coat on the floor and bursts into tears)*

[76] But we know perfectly well this isn't about the half-belt at all.

[77] Or imagine that you've been waiting for this moment your whole life.

[78] And now your heart is in your mouth as you push open the forbidden door...

[79] I.e., something like a tightly wound "goodbye forever."

[80] Is that clear?

[81]   So then, here I am!

[82]   ...here I am! I won't bore you, the
        reader, with the details of my
        exhausting trip...

[83]   ...the details of my exhausting trip,
        with descriptions of the people I
        happened to meet, some of whom were
        quite nice, while others I'd rather
        not even think about...

[84]   ...while others I'd rather not even
        think about, of the growing excitement
        and impatience as the coveted destina-
        tion comes closer...

[85] ...the growing excitement and
impatience as the coveted destination
comes closer, and so much besides...

[86] ...and so much besides. Now they're
barely distinguishable, they're fading
into the morning haze, these nighttime
visions...

[87] ...these nighttime visions, and now a
band of boisterous boys is racing down
the hill-side right to the river...

lev rubinstein

[88]   ...to the river, while the hills of the Rhine go rushing by, the castles and the vineyards...

[89]   ...the castles and the vineyards, and it all becomes so infinitely remote... the cracked teacup, the dusty stuffed squirrel, the glass marble, the crumpled piece of paper...

[90]   ...the glass marble, the crumpled piece of paper, and there is no sense any longer in beating the drum, it won't respond anyway because it's dead...

[91] ...it won't respond anyway because it's dead, and now the remains of a sad fire are crackling...

[92] ...the remains of a sad fire are crackling, but of course things cannot be disturbed...

[93] ...cannot be disturbed, and we go our separate ways...

lev rubinstein

[94]   We go our separate ways, don't forget
       me.

[95]   We go our separate ways, don't forget
       me.

[96]   We go our separate ways, don't forget
       me...

Glas New Russian Writing
contemporary Russian literature in English translation

GLAS BACK LIST

Peter Aleshkovsky, *Skunk: A Life,* a novel set in the Russian countryside
Ludmila Ulitskaya, *Sonechka*, a novel about a persevering woman
Asar Eppel, *The Grassy Street*, stories set in a Moscow suburb in the 1940s
Boris Slutsky, *Things That Happened*, poetry & biography of a major poet
The Portable Platonov, for the centenary of Russia's greatest writer
Leonid Latynin, *The Face-Maker and the Muse*, a novel-parable
Irina Muravyova, *The Nomadic Soul*, a novel about modern Anna Karenina
Anatoly Mariengof, *A Novel Without Lies*, the turbulent life of a great poet
    against the background of Bohemian Moscow in the flamboyant 1920s
Alexander Genis, *Red Bread*, Russian and American civilizations compared
    by Russia's foremost essayist
Larissa Miller, *Dim and Distant Days*, childhood in postwar Moscow
    recounted with sober tenderness and insight
Andrei Volos, *Hurramabad*, civil war in Tajikistan and fleeing Russians
Lev Rubinstein, *Here I Am*, humorous-philosophical sketches and poems
A.J.Perry, *Twelve Stories of Russia: a Novel I guess*, one American's
    adventures in today's Russia

COLLECTIONS

Revolution, the 1920s versus the 1980s
Soviet Grotesque, young people's rebellion against the establishment
Women's View, Russian woman bloodied but unbowed
Love and Fear, the two strongest emotions dominating Russian life
Bulgakov & Mandelstam, earlier autobiographical stories
Jews & Strangers, what it means to be a Jew in Russia
Booker Winners & Others, mostly provincial writers
Love Russian Style, Russia tries decadence
The Scared Generation, the grim background of today's ruling class
Booker Winners & Others-II, more samplings from the Booker winners
Captives, victors turn out to be captives on conquered territory
From Three Worlds, new Ukrainian writing
A Will & a Way, new women's writing
Beyond the Looking-Glas, Russian grotesque revisited
Chilldhood, the child is father to the man